Noodleheads See the Future

by Tedd Arnold
Martha Hamilton
and Mitch Weiss

illustrated by Tedd Arnold

Holiday House / New York

Specially for Grace,
who can often see the future!

HOLIDAY HOUSE is registered in the U.S. Patent and Trademark Office.
Printed and Bound in December 2017 at Toppan Leefung, DongGuan City, China.
The artwork was rendered digitally using Photoshop software.
www.holidayhouse.com
3 5 7 9 10 8 6 4 2

Library of Congress Cataloging-in-Publication Data

Names: Arnold, Tedd, author, illustrator. | Hamilton, Martha, author. | Weiss, Mitch, 1951- author.
Title: Noodleheads see the future / by Tedd Arnold, Martha Hamilton and Mitch Weiss ; illustrated by Tedd Arnold.
Description: First Edition. | New York : Holiday House, [2017] | Series: Early chapter book | Summary: Inspired by folktales about fools from around the world, brothers Mac and Mac Noodlehead exasperate Uncle Ziti, are fooled by their friend Meatball, and make a garden for their mother.
Identifiers: LCCN 2016004460 | ISBN 9780823436736 (hardcover)
Subjects: | CYAC: Fools and jesters—Fiction. | Brothers—Fiction. | Humorous stories.
Classification: LCC PZ7.A7379 Nu 2017 | DDC [E]—dc23 LC record available at https://lccn.loc.gov/2016004460

ISBN 978-0-8234-4014-6 (paperback)

I'm Mac!
And I'm Mac!
We're Noodleheads!
See in here? Nothing! Zippo! Nada!

Hey, Mac, there's Uncle Ziti.
Uncle Ziti, what are you doing?
Oh, hi, boys. I'm building a wall. Can you give me a hand?

What are you doing?
We would give you this hand.
But we can't get it off.
No. I mean... oh, never mind. Just listen up.

Okay.
Now what are you doing?
We are listening up.
I hear birds.

No! Look, it's a simple job. A piece of cake.
We love cake!
What kind?
I hope it's chocolate!
ARRGH! Just go home!

That's an easy job!
We can do that!
You think the cake is at home?
Maybe we get it when we finish this job!

NOODLEHEADS SEE THE FUTURE
CHAPTER 1
GETTING FIREWOOD
One day, Mac and Mac found their mother in the side yard.
What are you doing?

I can see a beautiful garden right here. Someday soon.
You can't see that. Because you can't see the future!
No one can see the future!

Maybe not. But I can dream.
Mac, whenever we help Mom, she bakes us a treat. We should help make her a garden!
Digging a garden is hard work!

True! We need to help her with an easy job. Hey, I know! We'll get firewood for the oven.
Then she can bake us a cake!
CAKE!
Let's go!

No firewood! We've been looking for hours!!!
Maybe we got it all last time.

Wait! I see some firewood up there.

SAW SAW SAW SAW
What's up?
Oh. Hi, Meatball.
We are up. Can't you see?

I can see that if you keep sawing you will soon fall down and bruise your bottoms.
You can't see that because you can't see the future.
No one can see the future.
And you don't know **anything** about getting firewood!
We will see about **that!**

SAW SAW SAW SAW SAW SAW SAW SAW SAW SAW SAW SAW SAW SAW SAW SAW
CRASH

OUCH! I bruised my bottom!
Me too!
Wait a minute. Meatball said this would happen.
You know what that means!

Meatball can see the future.

NOODLEHEADS SEE THE FUTURE
CHAPTER 2
THE TALKING DEAD
Meatball must be a fortune-teller!
I wonder what else he can see in our future.

LET'S GO ASK HIM!
Ask me what?
Oh, there you are.
Tell us our future.
You think I can see the future?

YES! You predicted that we would fall down...
...and bruise our bottoms. It all came TRUE!
Okay, you are right. I can see your future.
Tell us!

In one minute you will both be dead.

We better lie down...
...so we don't fall down when we die.
I'm closing my eyes.
Me too. I don't want to see us die.

Are you dead yet?
No.
How do you know?
I have an itch. I'm thinking dead people don't itch.

Dead people don't talk either!
WE AREN'T DEAD!
Meatball can't see the future!

Hey, where's our firewood?
MEATBALL!!!

There he is! He's trying to sneak away.
Hey, Meatball!
Who, me?
Are you **stealing** our firewood?
No, I am...um... trading you for something better.

Trading for what?
You give me this tiny pile of firewood...
...and I'll give you a big pile of magic firewood **seeds!**

What do we do with these?
Throw them in a hole, and POOF! Firewood will grow!

Thanks, Meatball! See ya later.
Sweet!
Magic firewood seeds are cool!
I can't wait to see the seeds go POOF!

NOODLEHEADS SEE THE FUTURE
CHAPTER 3
SEEING THE FUTURE
We will never have to go out to get firewood again!

WAIT!
Oh, no! I can see the future!
You can't see the...

Yes, I can! I see there will be no cake for us tonight.
Because we have no firewood.
But we have these firewood seeds. They go **POOF!**
Right?

Oh, right, I forgot. Okay! First, we dig a hole.
Now, throw in the seeds...
...and **POOF!**

...and POOF!

Hm-m-m.
What about this dirt pile?
It's right where Mom wants her beautiful garden.

I'll dig a hole and put that dirt in it.
There!
What about **this** pile of dirt?

I'll dig another hole.
There!
What about **that** dirt?

I'll dig another hole.
There!
What about **that** dirt?

Three hours later...
There!
What about **that** dirt?

WHAT?
What a beautiful garden you dug for me! What a lovely surprise! I will plant seeds right **now**!
seeds

WOW! Mom really can see the future!
She saw a beautiful garden, and here it is!

Digging a garden wasn't our surprise for Mom.
Firewood was our surprise.
I can see the future too.

We will have firewood soon.
Then we will have cake!

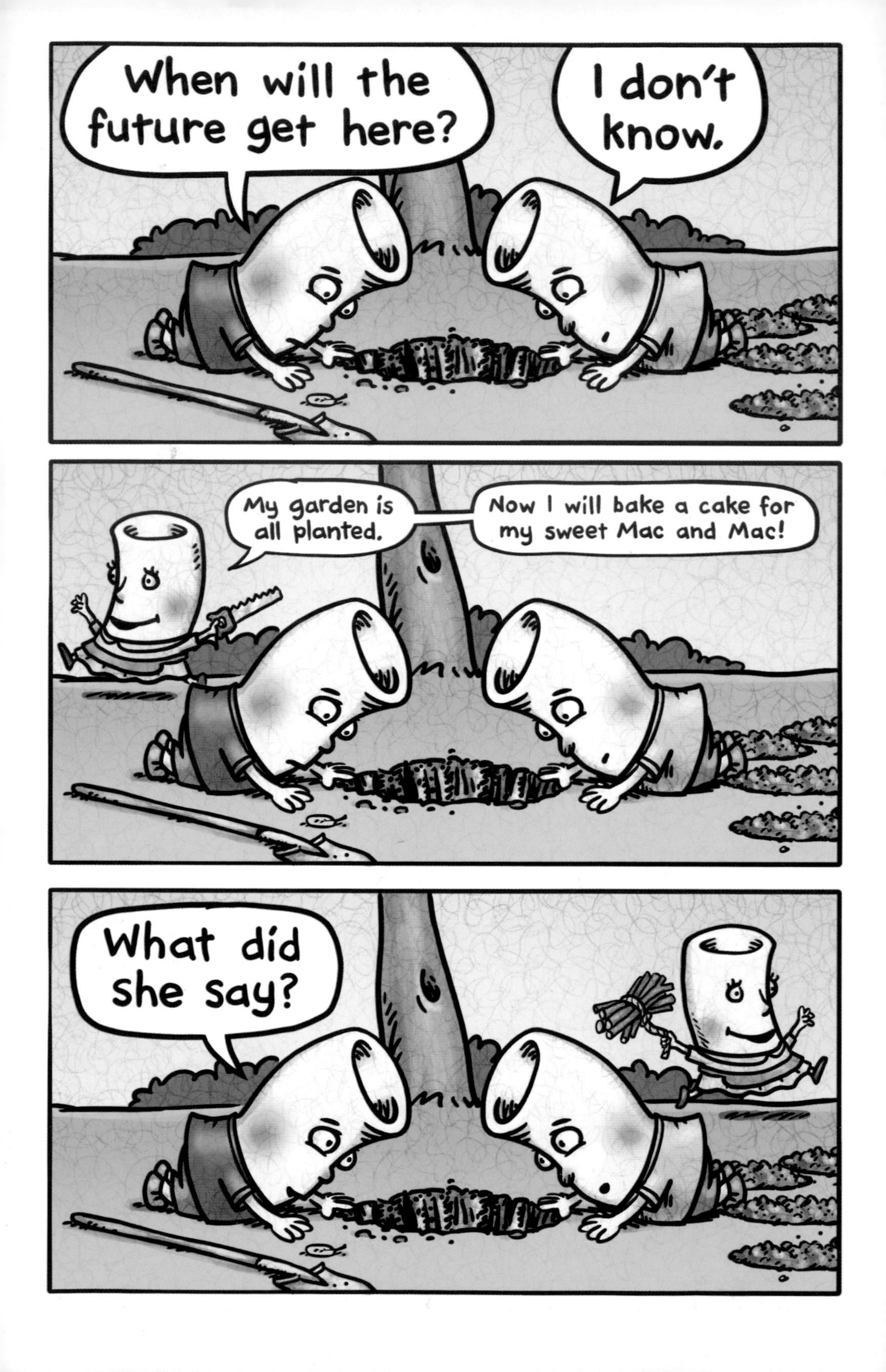
When will the future get here?
I don't know.
My garden is all planted.
Now I will bake a cake for my sweet Mac and Mac!
What did she say?

CAKE!
The future is here and it smells like cake!

Sometime in the future...